Gordon and Chase

In

The Curse of Montezuma's Mask
The Legend of the Stoddard Mine in Mayer, Arizona

Ghost Town Productions LLC
Copywrite © 2023; Richard G Johnson
All Rights Reserved

GHOST TOWN
PRODUCTIONS LLC

Prologue

It was November, 1519; Hernan Cortes, his Spanish soldiers and his 1,000 Tlaxcaltec warriors made it to Tenochtitlán, the Aztec capital. Montezuma met with Cortes to try and pay him off, however Cortes had his mind set on pillaging the Aztec capital for the Aztec gold and treasure. The Aztecs were great miners and metallurgists that had amassed and refined tons and tons of gold, silver, platinum and jade.

When Cortes declined the bribe, Montezuma declared that Cortes was sent by the god, Quetzalcatl and welcomed him to the city. The Spaniards were treated with great honor and Cortes took the opportunity to take Montezuma hostage. His plan was to rule the city through Montezuma.

However, in early 1520 Cortes learned of a Spanish force, led by Narváez to relieve him of his command. Cortes had to go to the coast to fight Panfilo de Narváez, a Spanish conquistador sent by the Governor of Cuba. While Cortes was fighting Narváez, the Aztecs had an uprising and killed his men. After defeating Narváez, Cortes realized that he did not have the army and weapons to defeat the Aztecs, so he escaped to the coast to sail back to Spain with a plan to return 12 months later with more men and weapons.

Montezuma knew Cortes would be back so he organized a 1000-man caravan and ordered his men to gather the Aztec Empire gold and treasure. Montezuma told his men to take the treasure North into what is now the American Southwest and hide it in several cave and mine locations.

Legend has it that the Aztec caravan made their way into present day Arizona and dug several intricate mines, for which to hide some of the Aztec treasure.

Table of Contents

Chapter 1

As the blazing sun beat down on the dusty terrain of 1912 Arizona, Gordon Johnson and his son, Chase Johnson, rode into a small town on horseback. Gordon, a rugged man with a weathered face and calloused hands, sat tall in his saddle, his eyes scanning the horizon for any sign of danger. Chase, a young man in his 20's, rode beside his father in silence. His eyes were taking in the unfamiliar sights and sounds of the Wild West.

As they entered the small town, Gordon tipped his hat to the few people who were out and about, his weather-beaten face giving away nothing of the journey they had endured to get here. Chase, on the other hand, couldn't contain his excitement. He looked around with wonder at the saloons, general stores, and stables that lined the dusty streets.

Gordon led the way to the town's livery stable, where they dismounted and tethered their horses. As they stepped into the shade of the stable, the he gave a nod of greeting to the grizzled old stable hand who was sitting in the shade, whittling a piece of wood.

"Good day, sir," Gordon said to the stable hand, his voice gruff but friendly. "I'm in need of some supplies and a place to stay for me and my boy. We are headed to California and need shelter for the night. Can you help us out?"

The stable hand looked up from his whittling and gave the father a once-over. After a moment, he nodded and said, "I reckon I can help you out, stranger."

"You can leave your horses here for 10 cents each. Then walk up to the Palace Saloon, they have good food and drink. Once you're done you can check with the Prescott Hotel for a room."

In the rugged landscape, father and son stood side by side, silhouetted against the warm glow of the setting sun. Chase's bright eyes shone with curiosity and eagerness, as he looked up at his father with a sense of admiration and awe. Though his frame was smaller than his father's, he held himself with a certain confidence that suggested he was eager to prove himself and follow in his father's footsteps.

Together, they stood in the midst of a vast expanse of wilderness, the rocky terrain stretching out before them as far as the eye could see. It was a rugged and unforgiving landscape, but the father and son were at home here, their spirits unbroken by the harsh realities of life in the Arizona Territory.

As the last rays of sunlight faded into the horizon, the father placed a reassuring hand on his son's shoulder, imparting the wisdom of generations past. Though they were but two small figures in an immense and untamed landscape, they were bound together by a love and respect that transcended time and space. For in that moment, they were not just father and son, but a testament to the enduring power of the human spirit.

"Son, life is all about what you put into it. And the adventure we're on right now is a test. It's a test to see if we are up for the challenge," Gordon said thoughtfully. "Are you up for the challenge that life is about to throw at you?"

Chase, knowing that his father was referring to their search for a mining claim to call their own, nodded, "I am…"

"Well, then there you have it!" Gordon replied, suddenly in a more cheerful mood.

Leading the way to the saloon in the center of town, Gordon whistled an upbeat melody as he tipped his hat to a rather dashing young lady making her way to the stables.

The saloon was a dimly-lit, smoky room, filled with the sounds of chatter, laughter, and the clinking of glasses. The bar was lined with row after row of bottles, and the air was thick with the smell of whiskey and beer.

Gordon ordered two glasses of whiskey while Chase sat down at a small table in the corner of the room. As they sipped their drinks, Gordon began to tell stories about his own youth. Chase listened intently, fascinated by his father's tales. He couldn't imagine his own life being so wild and free. As he took another sip of whiskey, he realized that his father was a man who had lived a full life, with all its ups and downs, and had come out the other side stronger for it.

As the night wore on, more patrons filtered in and out of the saloon, but Gordon and Chase remained at their table, lost in conversation. When they finally stood up to leave, Chase felt a sense of gratitude for his father. They were going to do great things together…

***

Prescott was a quaint town situated in the heart of the American West. The sun beat down on the dusty streets, where cowboys in wide-brimmed hats walked alongside businessmen in suits, and horse-drawn carriages shared the road with automobiles.

The town's centerpiece was the historic courthouse, an impressive structure made of red sandstone that loomed over the surrounding buildings. Its clock tower ticked away the hours as the townsfolk went about their daily business.

In the town square, a small market bustled with activity. Farmers sold fresh produce, while craftsmen hawked their wares.

The air was thick with the scent of roasting coffee and sizzling meats, and the sound of lively chatter filled the air.

Children played hopscotch and marbles in the shadow of the courthouse, and couples strolled hand-in-hand down the tree-lined streets. In the distance, the mountains loomed, a rugged and majestic backdrop to the peaceful town below.

As the day wore on, the streets began to empty as people retreated to their homes and businesses. The town settled into a peaceful calm, with only the occasional clip-clop of a horse's hooves or the distant cry of a coyote breaking the silence.

Tired and hungry, yet grateful to have made it to their destination, Gordon and Chase dismounted at the edge of the town, leading their horses by the reins as they made their way down the main street.

Gordon's eyes scanned the buildings on either side of him, looking for a place for them to rests their heads for the night. His gaze settled on a grand looking building with a sign that read "Prescott Hotel" hanging above the entrance.

They approached the hotel. The smell of fresh wood and leather greeted them as they made their way to the reception desk. A young woman with honey-colored hair stood behind the desk, a ledger in front of her.

"Good evening, sirs," she greeted them with a smile. "What can I do for you?"

"We're in need of a room for the night," Gordon replied, his voice a little rough from the long journey.

The young woman nodded; her pen poised over the ledger. "We have a few rooms available. May I have your names, please?"

The young woman made a notation in the ledger. She then reached under the desk and produced a key. "That will be $2."

Gordon paid the desk clerk. "Here you are, sir. Room 7. It's on the second floor, just down the hall to your left."

"Much obliged," Gordon replied, taking the key from her.

As they ascended the creaky wooden stairs to their room, both men marveled at the grandeur of the hotel. The walls were adorned with elegant wallpaper, and ornate sconces lined the hallways. Gordon opened the door to the room, revealing two comfortable beds and a small writing desk. The room was cool and airy, a welcome respite from the harsh desert sun outside.

Gordon sat down on the bed, yanked his boots off and placed them at the side of his bed. He then lay down with his wide-brim sheep-skin hat over his eyes. He listened to his son doing the same.

When it quieted down, Gordon sighed. Every night, before he closed his eyes, he thought of her and of that night when the world as he knew it came crashing down around him. He let the memory wash over him and take hold of his emotions.

That night, 10 years ago, the cold wind howled through the darkened streets as he stumbled, dazed and numb, through the deserted town. His mind was in a haze as he tried to make sense of what had just happened, but the reality was too painful to comprehend.

He had just lost the love of his life, his wife. She was riding home from the Albuquerque General Store and was robbed and murdered. The Sherriff found her body in the New Mexico desert several miles outside of town. The tragedy had left him with a grief that seemed to consume him entirely. Every breath felt like it took more effort than the last, as if the weight of his loss was crushing him.

Breaking the news to Chase, who was 12 years old at the time, stayed etched in his mind.

In the dimly-lit parlor of their modest home, Gordon sat his young son down and took a deep breath. The flickering flames of the coal stove cast shadows on the walls, lending an air of solemnity to the room.

"Son," he began, his voice heavy with grief. "I have some difficult news to share with you."

Chase looked up at his father, his eyes wide and expectant.

"Your mother, she's gone. She's gone to Heaven."

Gordon's voice broke as he spoke, and he took a moment to compose himself. Chase sat in silence, his mind struggling to comprehend the enormity of what he had just heard.

"She was a kind and gentle soul," Gordon continued, his words tinged with sadness. "Always there to comfort us, no matter how hard things got. But now, she's with the angels. Watching over us, guiding us, until we can be with her again."

Chase could see the pain etched deep in his father's eyes. But even in the midst of his own sorrow, Gordon remained strong for his son.

"We'll get through this, son," he said, his voice steady. "Together. We'll honor your mother's memory, and make sure she's never forgotten."

And with those words, Gordon and Chase sat in silence, the weight of their loss hanging heavy in the air. But even in the darkest of moments, they knew they had each other. And somehow, they would find a way to carry on.

In the days that followed after his wife's death, Gordon found himself wandering the quiet streets, unable to find any solace in the silence. Gordon felt an internal anger and guilt. The world around him continued on, as if nothing had happened, while he was left with a hole in his heart that seemed impossible to fill.

As Gordon let the memory of his late-wife fade while giving in to sleep taking his body, Chase lay awake.

It was something that had become part of his everyday life. Since his father never really spoke about Chase's mother, a lot was left unsaid.

Growing up without a mother was a daunting task for any child, especially Chase. It meant missing out on the gentle touch of a woman, the sweet scent of her perfume, and the sound of her soothing voice. It meant facing the world without the comfort and security of a mother's embrace, and learning to navigate life's challenges with an inner strength that few could comprehend.

It meant relying on the wisdom and guidance of fathers, aunts, grandmothers, or other female relatives to fill the void left by the absence of a mother's love. It meant learning to cook and clean at a young age, taking on responsibilities that were traditionally reserved for adults.

It also meant facing the stigma and shame of being an "unmothered child" in a society that placed a high value on motherhood. It meant enduring the pity and sympathy of others who saw the lack of a mother as a tragic loss, rather than a challenge to be overcome.

However, for Chase, it meant developing a fierce independence and resilience that served him well. It meant finding strength in his own inner resources, and learning to rely on himself when others let him down. It meant forging his own path in life, and proving to the world that he was just as capable, despite his unfortunate circumstances.

Chase, with his father's strength to guide him, reserved mourning for his mother in silent moments where no one could see the emotion connected to the feeling of loss. Together, without ever speaking a word about it, both father and son yearned for the one who they had lost too soon.

***

After his wife's death, Gordon continued working as a miner a mine nestled between the foothills near the town he grew up in. Since he was Chase's sole caregiver, he needed to work twice as hard to provide his son with the life his wife would have wanted him to have.

Day after day, for 10 years, he descended into the depths of the mine, the world above slowly fades away, replaced by a labyrinth of dimly-lit tunnels and passages. The air was thick with the smell of earth and rock, and the sound of distant machinery echoed off the walls.

His daily work began as he joined the crew of miners, each with their own tools and tasks to complete. Some were chipping away at the rock face with pickaxes, while others hauled heavy carts filled with ore. The work was hard and unrelenting, with little room for error or hesitation.

As Gordon worked, he felt the weight of the world above him pressing down, a constant reminder of the danger and unpredictability of the mine. He had to be alert at all times, listening for any sign of danger, from the creak of a support beam to the rumble of an approaching collapse.

But despite the challenges, there was a sense of camaraderie among the miners, a shared bond born of the hardships they endured each day. However, Gordon felt the need to leave the known behind and travel into the unknown. At times, he thought that it might be his own way of running from his reality. But the more he thought about it, the more it made sense. And it would give Chase the opportunity to grow into a confident young man who knows that hard work pays off.

On some days, he was able to take Chase along with him to earn his keep alongside his father. And since Chase looked much older than he was, the company Gordon worked for did not look too far into the matter as long as they had an extra pair of hands to handle the hard labor while paying as little as possible.

While working alongside his father and other rugged miners, Chase learned to be precise, confident and quickly caught onto the way miners thought about their lives.

On one particular day, Gordon wiped his forehead as he looked at the mine wall in front of him, "It's a hot one down here today. How's the drilling going?"

Chase said, "It's slow going, as usual. But we're making some progress. I think the vein is getting wider."

Gordon nodded, proud of the progress his son was making, "That's good news. We could use a bit of luck down here. I was talking to some of the other miners, and they're saying that the demand for silver and gold is going up. This means the price for both will be increasing."

"Really? That's great. Maybe we'll finally get a raise then," Chase said, trying to sound as important as the other miners around him.

Gordon shook his head, "I wouldn't count on it, son. The company is always looking to cut costs, and they know we're all desperate to keep our jobs."

"I know, it's not fair. They make all the profits, and we do all the hard work. It's about time we stood up for ourselves," Chase continued.

"I understand how you feel, but we have to be careful," Gordon put a hand on his son's shoulder while wondering if he had made the right choice by exposing his son to the harsh reality of mining. "If we push too hard, we could end up losing our jobs or worse. We have to pick our battles."

Chase sighed, "I know, you're right. It's just frustrating. It feels like we're stuck down here, working ourselves to the bone for nothing."

"I know, it's not an easy life," Gordon answered. "We both know that. But we have each other, and we have our health. That's something to be grateful for."

"Yeah, you're right. We make a good team, don't we?" Chase said, suddenly less frustrated.

"We certainly do. And who knows, maybe someday we'll strike it rich and we can retire!" Gordon joked.

"I like the sound of that. But until then, we'll just have to keep digging," Chase mused as he mucked ore into the ore cart.

Gordon looked at his son – tired, sweaty and full of dirt. Yes, they had to keep drilling. But not for long…

Gordon had a plan to sell his house with all furnishings. He would pack up his two colt peacemakers, the gold nuggets he had been saving for decades and other supplies. His plan was to travel to California to purchase a mining claim. But in order for his plan to work, he needed to obtain as much information as he possibly could to ensure they'd get a profitable claim.

The process for obtaining a mining claim in the United States was governed by the General Mining Law of 1872. The law allowed any citizen of the United States or those who have declared their intention to become a citizen to explore, locate and claim valuable mineral deposits on federal public lands.

To obtain a mining claim, Gordon would first need to identify a potential site where minerals were likely to be found. Once a location was found, he would need to go to the local land office in the county where the claim was located, and file a Notice of Location for the claim.

The Notice of Location would include the name of the claim, the location, and the type of mineral that was being sought. It would also need to be filed with the county recorder or other local land office.

He would then need to stake the claim by placing posts or markers at the corners of the claim to identify the boundaries. The size of a mining claim was limited to 20 acres in size, and each corner post or marker had to be visible from the others.

After staking the claim, he would need to file a claim with the local land office within 30 days, which would require paying a fee. The claim would then be recorded in the office and he would receive a certificate of ownership, which would provide legal recognition of the claim.

While on route to California, Gordon and Chase often attempted panning for gold at designated riverbeds.

The price of gold was increasing as father and son prospectors headed out into the rugged, untamed desert, with nothing but a pickaxe, a pan, and a dream. Panning for gold was a tough, backbreaking job, but for those who could consistently wash rocks and find gold, it was worth all the effort.

They arrived at the bank of a rushing stream, its crystal-clear waters glistening in the morning light. Gordon kneeled down, his weathered hands expertly digging into the soft soil, as he explained the basics of gold panning to his eager son.

Gordon taught his son how to dip the pan into the water, carefully washing away the dirt and sediment to reveal any glimmers of gold. As the hours passed, they honed their technique, discovering that the key to success was patience and persistence.

They dug deeper and sifted through the gravel, their eyes fixed on the prize of striking it rich.

Finally, after what felt like an eternity, their efforts paid off. A glimmering nugget caught their eye, shining like a beacon of hope amidst the murky water. Gordon beamed with pride, their hard work and determination finally rewarded.

The work was hard, but there was something exhilarating about the search for gold. Every swirl of the pan brought the possibility of riches beyond imagining, and the hope of striking it big kept the prospectors going. As the day wore on, the sun beat down on their backs, and the icy water numbed their fingers, but still they persisted, determined to find their fortune.

Although they did not find large amounts of gold, it was a welcoming add to their savings kept aside for the purchase of the right mining claim.

Chapter 2

As Gordon and his son stepped through the swinging doors of the Palace Saloon in Prescott, eager to enjoy a well-deserved meal, the smell of whiskey and tobacco hit them like a punch in the gut. The dimly lit room was filled with a haze of smoke, making it difficult to see the other side of the room.

The walls of the Palace Saloon were lined with bottles of every shape and size, each filled with a different kind of liquor. The bar itself stretched almost the entire length of the bar room, polished to a shine despite years of use. The bartender was a grizzled old-timer, his face weathered by years in the sun and the occasional brawl.

In one corner of the saloon, a group of cowboys were engaged in a heated game of poker. The sound of shuffling cards and clinking chips mixed with the murmur of conversation made it difficult to hear anything clearly. The air was thick with tension as each player tried to outsmart the others and walk away with a handful of cash.

At the other end of the room, a piano player hammered away at the keys, providing a lively soundtrack to the scene. The wooden floorboards creaked underfoot as patrons shuffled around, looking for a place to sit or standing at the bar, eager to quench their thirst.

Despite the rowdy atmosphere, there was a sense of camaraderie in the air. The Palace Saloon may have been a place where fights break out and fortunes were won and lost, but it was also a place where people came to forget their troubles and enjoy the company of others.

Gordon and Chase settled down at a table in the far corner of the saloon. The table was sticky with spilled beer and covered in dust, but they were too hungry to care. Gordon flagged down a server, a young woman with a tray balanced expertly on one hand.

"What can I get for you?" she asked, her voice barely audible over the din.

The choices were simple but satisfying: steak, potatoes, beans, and cornbread. Both father and son decided on a steak, medium-rare, with a side of beans and cornbread.

The server took a mental note, then disappeared into the throng of patrons.

It did not take long for the server to reappear while balancing a steaming plate of food in each hand. She set the order down in front of the men, the sizzle of the steak audible over the noise. Thanking her, Gordon cut into the meat, the juices running down his knife and onto the plate. Chase ate eagerly, musing over the rich and savory beans as well as the moist cornbread.

After finishing their meal, Gordon's eye kept catching a glimpse of a man sitting at the bar. Every once in a while, men would approach him cautiously and respectfully while exchanging a few words. Then, they would quickly make their way out of the saloon. It was clear that the man sitting at the bar hunched over a glass of amber liquid was a man of power.

He wore a wide-brimmed hat pulled low over his forehead, and his weathered face was etched with lines of experience. Intrigued, Gordon motioned for Chase to follow him as he made his way over to the bar.

The man glanced over at Gordon as he ordered a drink. His eyes seemed to carry with them an unsettling atmosphere.

Before Gordon could introduce himself, the man said, his gaze steady. "Name's Celord Stoddard."

Shaking his hand, Gordon introduced himself and his son, "Nice to meet you." Pausing, Gordon started saying, "Stoddard…"

The Stoddard Copper Company was primarily involved in the mining of copper, gold, and silver. Its main operations were located in the Bisbee area, which was one of the most productive mining districts in the Arizona Territory at the time. The Stoddard Mining Company owned several mines in the area, including the Stoddard Mine, Copper Queen, the Copper King, and the Queen of Bisbee. What's more, the Stoddard Mining Company was one of the largest and most successful mining companies in Arizona. It employed hundreds of workers and produced millions of dollars' worth of copper, gold and silver each year.

Gordon could hardly believe his luck.

"Yes," Celord mused, knowing that his last name carried stature and authority as most people regarded him to be a very rich and powerful man. "What brings you to Prescott?" Celord asked.

"My son and I are just passing through, really," Gordon replied.

"Ah, don't let the simplicity of Prescott fool you," Celord smiled. "There is much more to this piece of paradise than you might imagine…"

Gordon listened attentively as Celord talked about the town and its hidden features.

The town itself was made up of a series of streets, which were laid out in a grid pattern. Most of the buildings in the town were made of ponderosa pine, as this was the most prevalent tree in the area.

According to Celord, Prescott was the center of the Arizona mining industry, and many of its residents were involved. Prescott was the Territory Capital. The town was also a hub for cattle ranching, which was an important part of the local economy and also had a number of small businesses, including general stores, bakeries, and blacksmith shops. It also had several government buildings, including a courthouse, a jail, and a governor's mansion.

The courthouse was a large, impressive building that dominated the town square.

"It was built in the Classical Revival style and featured a grand entrance with large columns," Celord knowingly commented.

To Gordon, it was clear that Celord's roots lay deep within Prescott and although he had a sly look about him, it amused Gordon to see a man talk about his home town with such pride.

Despite its small size, Gordon was surprised to find out that the town had social clubs and organizations. These included a Women's Club, which was dedicated to promoting women's rights and improving the community, and a Rotary Club, which was focused on community service. The town also had several saloons and other establishments where residents could socialize.

The town also had a public library, which was housed in a small building on one of the main streets. The library was open to everyone in the community and was a popular gathering spot for residents.

However, one of the most important industries was mining. Many men worked in the mines extracting copper, silver, gold and other minerals from the surrounding mountains. Others worked in related industries such as smelting, refining, and transportation.

Cattle ranching were another important industry in Prescott. The town was located in an area that was well-suited to raising cattle, and many ranches were established in the surrounding countryside. Men who worked in the ranching industry were responsible for everything from raising and caring for the animals to driving them to market.

Lawyers, judges, and politicians were all common professions in the town, as were jobs in law enforcement and other government agencies. Men who worked in government jobs played a key role in shaping the policies and laws of the territory, and they helped to establish Prescott as an important political center in the region.

As Celord entertained them with banter about the town, Gordon had another idea play in his mind.

Would it be wise to tell Stoddard of his intention to buy a claim? Would Stoddard be able to provide him with advice as to which claims might be more profitable? Why would a highly-regarded man like Stoddard even be interested in talking to someone like him?

Thoughts ran through Gordon's head as he contemplated what to say next.

Celord, with the notion that the newcomers should take his hospitality with a pinch of salt, quickly added, "Which is why you'd better make it very clear what your business with Prescott is. We wouldn't want any casualties..."

Still trying to determine whether Celord was being sincere or just plain rude, Gordon explained, "We're on our way to California. Looking to stake or buy a mining claim there..."

Celord's entire mood changed from purposefully toying with Gordon to focusing his full attention on the man sitting beside him. He set his glass down on the counter and faced the father and son; a small grin spreading across his face.

"So, you're interested in buying a mining claim..." Celord murmured.

"I am. I hear there's a fortune to be made in those parts of the world," Gordon nodded.

Celord smiled, "My dear friend, it has to be fate that brought you here, then. And here I thought you were just another passer-by looking to make a fortune from other's hard work..."

Producing a rather weathered map from his pocket, he unfolded it and placed it on the bar in front of them. Gordon looked down at the yellow paper. It had a few creases and patches of dry dirt but what was illustrated on it, is what caught his attention. Chase, too, moved closer to get a better look.

"This is in the Mayer area. You probably rode close to these claims to get here." Celord explained. A map surveying 8 patented claims along the Agua Fria River owned by the Stoddard Copper Company stared back at him. Gordon glanced at the man sitting beside him before looking back at the map on the bar counter.

"See this claim over here?" Stoddard asked as he pointed toward a rectangular survey with the words Copper Outlet written on it. "The Copper Outlet Claim is rich in copper, silver and gold. And it just so happens that the Stoddard Mining Company is looking to sell the claim…"

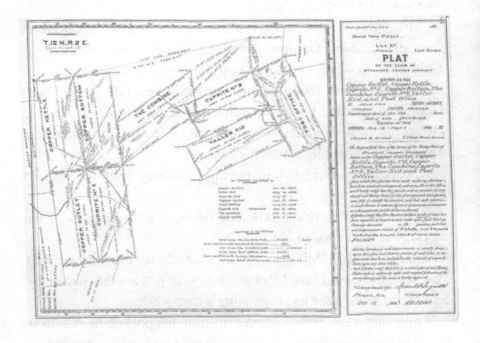

Celord let his voice trail off for effect. He could see Gordon salivating over the prospect of purchasing a claim like the one stipulated on the map.

"Astounding… Could you tell me a little more about the claim?" Gordon asked eagerly, pushing the uneasy feeling he was getting to the back of his mind.

"Well, of course!" Celord smiled, squaring his shoulders to show he was in full-business mode. "It's located in a prime location and has a history of yielding large quantities of ore. Proven to produce at an alarmingly prosperous pace, there are a lot of interested parties willing to partake in the race to riches! We started to follow a large vein into the mountain on the claim but decided to focus our efforts on a neighboring claim.

"It sounds like any miner's dream!" Chase chimed in, barely able to keep his excitement at bay.

Gordon, not wanting to get ahead of himself, cleared his throat, "What is your asking price for this claim?"

Since the claim was part of the Stoddard Copper Company's legacy, Gordon was sure the price would exceed anything and everything he would be able to give. Which is why when he heard Celord's response, he accidently knocked a glass of liquid out onto the map on the counter.

Jumping into action, Gordon picked the map up and apologized for his clumsiness. Celord, on the other hand, was beaming. He had Gordon exactly where he wanted him…

"$300 is a fair price, I suppose, for a proven claim," Gordon uttered.

It would be hard to part with a significant amount of his savings he had collected while mining over the past several years. However, if he was going to commit to purchasing the claim, he would need to see if it was worth the money, himself. Prospecting would show him the way forward.

"So we are interested, but we need to see the claim for ourselves and do a little testing." Celord nodded his head and said "I'll give you two days."

Perhaps their fortunes lay in the underground of Mayer, Arizona. Although it was a small town with a population of around 500 people, the area itself promised fortune to those who were willing to work for it.

Chapter 3

The sun was just beginning to peek over the mountains as the horses were saddled up. Gordon and Chase, well-rested and excited to see where the day's journey would take them, rode in silence while listening to their horse's hooves dipping into the streets of Prescott.

As they made their way out of town, the men were greeted by the breathtaking beauty of the Arizona landscape. Rolling hills, the smell of junipers, and dusty trails stretched out before them, beckoning them onward. The riders urged their horses into a steady trot, the rhythmic sound of their hooves on the ground creating a symphony of motion.

Gordon, hopeful that the Copper Outlet Claim would be kind to their prospecting mission, couldn't help but smile. Everything was working out so well. Yes, mining had its own hardships but the reward was worth the fight.

"Father, will you purchase the claim if it yields enough gold?" Chase asked as he steadied his horse.

"Son, I would not have agreed to ride 18 miles East of Prescott had I not thought every possible outcome through," Gordon said. "Stoddard, if he is the kind of man I hope he is, won't beat around the bush when it comes to money."

"So we're not going to California, are we?" Chase questioned.

"If there is something you want to say, boy, you need to say it," Gordon muttered, feeling a little frustrated with his son's sudden unenthusiastic approach to where they were headed.

"I… Something just doesn't sit right… Why would a man like Stoddard want to sell a claim for such little money? Especially if the claim has proven to be dotted with gold. Given his stature, it would only seem wise to sell it to the highest bidder," Chase thought out loud.

"You clearly still have a lot to learn..." Gordon replied, dismissing his son's thoughts.

However, he had to admit that Stoddard had been overly keen to sell them the claim. Deciding to push the uncomfortable thoughts from his mind, he laughed and said, "Oh, come on, son. We have an entire day of prospecting ahead of us!"

Chase, who cheered up at the thought of panning alongside his father for potential treasure, started whistling a tune as they neared the claim boundary.

Celord had explained that the claim contained a drift that seemed to have caved in on itself and as Gordon and Chase neared the particular sight in question, they couldn't help but wonder what had caused the cave-in in the first place. However, mining is dangerous work and it was not uncommon to hear of miners trapped and left for dead while unearthing minerals.

Then they began by carefully selecting a spot on the mining claim that looked promising; there were a couple flat spots that seemed to have been leveled out by previous mining activity. There was a spring for water just 500 yards from the caved in mine entrance. They grabbed some burlap sacks and started picking into what looked to be a vein that the other miners were following. They crushed the ore then loaded in their burlap to take to the spring to pan.

With a flick of his wrist, Gordon swirled the pan around, letting the water and gravity do their work. The lighter, useless material floated to the surface, leaving behind a layer of heavier, darker grains that could be the key to their purchase.

Following his father's lead, Chase carefully poured off the water, revealing a layer of sand and rocks at the bottom of his own pan. His heart raced as he sifted through the contents, hoping to find a glimmer of Gold.

"Will you look at that!" Gordon smiled as he picked at something in his pan. "We have not even properly started yet and it seems we have found our very first gold nugget!"

At the sight of the small, yet promising mineral pinched between his father's fingers, Chase forgot all about the uneasy feeling that followed him all the way from Prescott. Watching the expression on his father's face was enough to make him realize that they might have found what they were looking for after all.

Swopping their pans of a dry sluice test, they begin to sift through the layers of sand and gravel that make up the claim. Carefully separating the heavier minerals from the lighter ones, they gradually worked their way through the layers to uncover the hidden treasures beneath.

It was settled. Celord's words were true. This mining claim contained copper, gold and silver

With their findings as proof, Gordon and Chase prepared for the journey to Celord's office at the Stoddard Copper Company.

While trotting along a dirt road that separated the Copper Claim from another claim owned by Stoddard, Gordon and Chase were alerted to the sound of men talking in raised voices. On the other side of a marked fence, a group of men seemed to become more irate by the second.

From what the men were shouting toward each other, Gordon came to the conclusion that the claim, which had been discovered by a prospector named Gail, contained a rich vein of gold and silver, and had attracted the attention of several other miners who were eager to get their hands on the treasure.

As tensions rose between Gail and the other miners, it became clear that a violent clash was inevitable. On a scorching hot day, in the middle of the dusty desert, the two sides faced off against each other.

At first, the conflict was verbal, with the miners shouting insults and threats at each other.

Gordon slowed his horse to a walk as he heard one of the men shout, "This is my claim, boys. I've been working this land for months, and I won't let any of you take it from me."

Another man replied in disgust, "You don't own this land, and you don't own that claim. We have just as much right to it as you do."

"Who made you king of the desert?" A third man spat, "We're all out here trying to make a living, and you're not going to hog all the riches for yourself."

The man, who was adamant that the claim belonged to him, tried to explain, "I'm not trying to hog anything. I staked this claim fair and square, and I've put in the hard work to make it productive. I won't let you take that away from me."

"Well, you're going to have to fight for it, Gail. We're not going to just hand it over to you," the first man threatened.

Gail nodded, "I'm not afraid to fight for what's mine. But I warn you, if you try to take this claim by force, I'll defend it with everything I've got."

"We're not afraid of you, Gail," the second man added, "We've got just as much grit as you do. Let's settle this once and for all."

Gail threw a pickaxe he clutched in his hand on the dirt, "Fine by me. I'll defend my claim with everything I've got. But you'd better be ready for a fight because I won't go down without a fight."

Suddenly, the sound of fists hitting flesh echoed through the arid landscape as the miners began to fight. Picks and shovels were soon drawn, turning the fight into a deadly struggle. The sound of metal clanging against metal filled the air, as the miners swung their tools at each other with wild abandon.

Gordon and Chase, who watched the brawl unfold from a safe distance, were used to fights like these. To them, it seemed unlikely that either side would gain a clear advantage. However, Gail, who was outnumbered, fought fiercely to protect his claim. Unfortunately, his opponents were overwhelming.

Just when it seemed like Gail was about to be overrun, a group of local lawmen came trotting up on the dirt road. They had been tipped off about the fight and had ridden out to intervene. Their arrival had a calming effect on the situation, and the miners slowly began to back off. The lawmen even managed to separate the two sides and restore some order to the chaos.

Despite the intervention of the lawmen, the fight had taken a toll on both sides. Several miners were injured, with cuts and bruises covering their bodies. Gail, who had fought with everything he had, was left battered but victorious. The mining claim, however, remained a source of contention between the two sides, and it was clear that the conflict was far from over.

As Gordon gestured toward his son, he said, "It's not always going to be easy... Use what you saw today and let it be a lesson you can use during your life."

Following his father down the road away from the now-calm situation, Chase frowned, "Lesson?"

Gordon just smiled and replied, "One day you'll understand."

***

With their findings carefully folded between layers of cloth and tucked securely into their pockets, Gordon and Chase made their way to the Stoddard Copper Company where they were to meet with Celord Stoddard himself.

The structure, constructed of rough-hewn timber, stood tall against the stark desert landscape, a symbol of the determination and grit of the men who worked within its walls.

As they approached the office, the sound of stamping machines and the clanging of pickaxes could be heard in the distance, a constant reminder of the backbreaking labor that took place just beyond its doors. The entrance was adorned with a sign bearing the name of the mine and a warning to all who entered: "Danger, Keep Out."

Inside, the office was dimly lit, the only source of light coming from a few small windows that struggled to let in the scorching Arizona sun. The air was thick with the scent of sweat, gunpowder, and the faint hint of coffee. The walls were lined with shelves filled with dusty ledgers and mining maps, each one a testament to the hard work and dedication of the miners who risked their lives in pursuit of precious metals.

The sound of typewriters clacking and telegraphs buzzing filled the room, as clerks and bookkeepers meticulously recorded every detail of the mine's daily operations. The manager's desk, located at the front of the room, was adorned with a leather-bound ledger and a revolver, a constant reminder of the dangers that came with the job.

On the other side of the desk sat Stoddard, smiling as if anticipating their visit. Without getting up from his chair, he gestured toward Gordon and Chase to take a seat.

"I do hope you found what you were looking for, Stoddard greeted.

Placing the cloth rags in front of Stoddard, Chase opened them to reveal several large chunks of copper and silver oxide as well as a few very small gold nuggets.

"Promising, don't you think?" Celora added with his head reeling around the business side of the deal he was about to make.

"In all my years of mining, I have never encountered such adequate finds upon the first test!" Gordon mused, feeling excitement take over.

"Then we'd better make it official," Celord said as he opened a ledger to a clean page and began to write without giving Gordon the chance to voice his acceptance of purchasing the claim.

As he wrote, Celord glanced at Chase, "Young man, did you know that mining played a significant role in the development of Arizona in the 1800s? The discovery of rich mineral deposits, particularly copper, led to a mining boom that brought thousands of people to this territory in search of fortune."

Chase nodded, "Yes, Sir. My father taught me well."

"Good lad," Celord mused as he continued talking, "Mining is often a dangerous and difficult occupation, with miners working long hours in challenging conditions. However, it is also a lucrative industry, and many people are able to make a good living from mining."

"Which is why we are thrilled to be dealing with the Stoddard Copper Company," Gordon added.

Ignoring his statement, Celord continued writing and, almost as if lost in thought, said, "The Stoddard Copper Company is a major player in the Arizona mining industry. The company was founded by my father, William Stoddard, who had previously worked as a mining engineer in California. My father arrived in Arizona in the late 1870s and began exploring the copper deposits in the region. He eventually acquired several mining claims in the Clifton-

Morenci area, which were known for their high-quality copper ore. He then established the Stoddard Copper Company in 1880 and began mining operations in the area. The company quickly became one of the largest copper producers in the state, with a workforce of hundreds of miners and a network of smelters and refining facilities. One of the company's most significant achievements was the construction of a 32-mile-long narrow-gauge railway that connected the Morenci mine to the Southern Pacific Railroad… So you see, the success of this company means a lot to me…"

Finding Celord's last words a little threatening, Gordon exchanged a leather bag with money for an official document stating that he was the rightful claim owner of Copper Outlet Mining Claim.

"I look forward to doing business with you again," Celord said as he stood up from his desk, shaking hands with Gordon and then Chase.

Tipping their hats, both father and son stepped out into the sunlight.

Chapter 4

"Hand me that shovel, will you?" Gordon asked as he wiped the sweat from his dirty forehead.

Chase stumbled over a few boulders to get to the shovel in question. He was exhausted. But they had to finish the day's work. He squinted into the setting sun as he handed his father the tool.

It had been nearly two months since they had purchased the mining claim from Celord Stoddard. And it was an interesting claim, to say the very least. With much discussion, Gordon had decided to open the caved-in part of the drift. Since someone had clearly mined there in the past, the drift had to hold something valuable.

Like a pirate on the scent of a treasure chest full of gold, Gordon feverishly began the task of clearing the drift. While he was moving rocks with the help of a few hired miners, Chase sluiced the dirt at the entrance of the mine to ensure they didn't miss anything. It was a grueling process but since the drift entrance ran across a rich vein of gold, silver and copper, it made the endless hours of work worthwhile.

"Father!" Chase yelled as his eyes suddenly settled on something odd in the sluice box. "I think you'd better come and see this."

Gordon handed his shovel to the miner standing next to him and instructed him to keep clearing the area. With hope in his eyes, he walked over to the rusty sluice box where his son stood; pointing at something in the dirt.

Poking through the dirt, Gordon's fingers touched something rigid and elongated. As he picked it up, he inspected it.

"Not what I expected…" he muttered, hoping to see a large nugget. Instead, he held what looked like a bone fragment.

"I found three more of these today," Chase confirmed while pointing to a small pile of what looked like chicken bones.

"Could be some sort of mammal… Or a reptile perhaps…"

He handed the fragment back to Chase while adding, "If you discover more of these fragments, place them in this box."

Chase took the wooden box his father handed him and nodded. Without thinking too much about it, Gordon went back to clearing the drift.

As the days wore on, it became clear that the Copper Outlet had much to offer. Large chunks of gold made their appearance. Gordon was able to pay the hired miners, maintain the second-hand mining equipment he gathered and still had enough left to feed both himself and his son. Within another month, it seemed like they were well on their way to having a successful mining operation.

"Can you smell it?" Gordon asked one morning as he stood beside his son at the cleared-out drift. "The smell of decayed earth is quite strong here… If we move these two boulders, we might just stand a chance at opening the original drift!"

Feeding off his father's excitement, Chase chipped away at a large rock while his father assisted a few miners. Together, they trucked silver ore to the stamp mill and smelter.

Within a few hours, Gordon, Chase and the miners got their first taste of the original mine drift. With a small opening leading into a tunnel-like cavity, it took a lot of pushing and shoving to get into the cramped space. Everyone was in awe.

Gordon shook hands with one of the miners, elated to have such hard-working people at his side. He slapped Chase on the back and smiled from ear to ear. Everyone was excited that they might have a virgin vein to follow which should be much more lucrative than the mining the cave in overburden.

More rocks were moved away from the inside of the mine, making it easier to move around without the danger of having it cave in once more. To ensure the safety of the tunnel, large wooden posts were pressed up against the cave floor and ceiling.

"Halt! Everyone halt!" a miner yelled as he stepped back from a rock he had just lifted.

"What is the matter?" Gordon asked as he walked over to the miner.

For a few moments, he didn't say a word. Before him, on the ground, lay the distinctive features of a human skull. With a pungent, stagnate smell in the dank air. The group hesitantly entered a larger chamber. Once in the chamber with their miner lamps and a few large torches Gordon counted another 21 human skulls. A few scattered bones lay next to it – a femur, a spine and what was left of a foot. Kneeling beside the sight cautiously, Gordon looked at the remains. As Gordon lit up the cavern, he saw what looked to be 20 or more completely decomposed skeletons.

"Father, is it…" Chase couldn't get himself to say the words out loud.

"It seems like it," Gordon confirmed, also not saying the words directly. Then, clearing his throat, he got up and glanced at the area they were standing in. "They seem to be human remains… And judging from the level of decomposition, I would estimate these to be at least 300 – 400 years old."

"Something is amiss here," Chase said as he took a closer look at the remains. "Surely, we've just stumbled upon a casualty of the mine."

"I am not so sure about that. I think there is more to this than a simple cave in. I'd like to talk to Stoddard about this. Perhaps he could shine some light on the matter," Gordon said.

The next day, as Gordon explained what he saw in the mine, Celord shifted from one foot to the other in his office.

"And you are sure these are of human origin?" Celord asked.

"I do not mean to be rude but I have seen my fair share of death to know the difference between human and animal remains," Gordon answered.

"I am not sure what you are trying to imply but I can assure you, whatever you think you know is in no way at all a possibility," Celord said with sudden frustration. "Better you just keep sluicing and keep your findings to yourself. We don't want to attract any unwanted attention, do we?"

Gordon thought about the implications of government intervention or having unwarranted miners wanting to get their hands on the content of Copper Outlet. He surely didn't want that. But to him, it was clear that Celord was hiding something. He couldn't put his finger on it quite yet but there was something bothering the otherwise unbothered man…

***

Patrick McGill, claim owner and mining boss at Copper Queen and Binghamton mines was a figure to be reckoned with. He was a towering presence amidst the dust and grime of the mines. A man who commanded respect and obedience from his subordinates, he instilled a sense of discipline and order in the chaotic world of underground mining.

Owning most of the mining claims in and around Prescott and Mayer, he thoroughly enjoyed control over the mines and the workers who mined them. The world was abuzz with innovation and industry, and in the midst of it all stood McGill, a cunning businessman. He was a man of sharp wit and clever strategy, always one step ahead of his competitors. Always in a three-piece suit, complete with a bowler hat and polished shoes, he carried himself with an air of confidence and sophistication. His eyes were sharp and calculating, constantly scanning the room for opportunities and potential threats.

He was a master of negotiation and persuasion, able to sway even the most stubborn of clients to his side. He had a silver tongue, and his words were laced with a subtle charm that made it impossible to say no to him. But behind his charming façade lay a ruthless ambition. He was willing to do whatever it took to get ahead, even if it meant playing dirty. He was a master of deception, able to manipulate others into doing his bidding without them even realizing it. His business acumen was unmatched, and he was able to turn even the smallest investment into a massive profit.

"Pardon, Sir. I have obtained information I think you might find valuable," one of Patrick's informants said as he entered the boss's office with his hat in his hands.

"Have you discovered the biggest gold nugget the West has seen thus far?" Patrick asked sarcastically while blowing smoke into the air as he took a puff of his cigar.

With a solemn look on his face, the informant stood still, unsure of what to say or do next. Patrick, who usually took his time playing games with those he came in contact with, was curious to know what the man had to say.

"Sit down, take a break. You certainly earned it if you so urgently needed to see me," Patrick added.

Thank you, Sir..." the informant sat down in the chair opposite Patrick and dusted off his pants while laying his hat over his knee. "It seems that a certain Celord Stoddard has sold the Copper Outlet."

"How certain are you about this?" Patrick asked, a dark cloud suddenly obscuring his demeanor.

"Fairly certain, Sir. The Stoddard Mining Company confirmed it," the informant continued, hoping that the information he just provided would give him extra authority.

Patrick sat on his side of the desk for a few minutes without saying a single word. The informant started fidgeting; feeling uncomfortable.

Suddenly, Patrick jumped up and threw the stacks of paper files from his desk. A glass of half-empty whiskey crashed to the floor and an ashtray filled with cigar ash broke into two pieces at the side of the table.

The sudden rage in Patrick caught the informant off-guard as he stepped back from his seat.

"Get out!" Patrick yelled.

Not waiting for Patrick to say anything else, the informant sprinted out the door, thankful to get out of the situation alive.

McGill's untimely enraged episodes had made him somewhat of a scary man to be around. Everyone who was anyone knew that it was best to stay out of Patrick's way when he was angry; which was most of the time.

Patrick paced the room while stepping over the broken glass. He breathed heavily as his mind reeled over what he had just heard.

Celord sold the claim without his knowledge. Patrick and Celord had always had a very clear understanding with each other that all mining claim sales, ran through McGill first. It filled him with rage to know that Celord would bypass his judgement without consulting with him first. And, as per their agreement, a certain percentage of funds generated through claims sold were rightfully Patrick's. It seemed like Celord had intentionally kept the selling of the Copper Outlet a secret so he could keep all of the proceeds.

Merely thinking about Celord misusing his trust made him even angrier. Capsizing his chair, he screamed in a fiery rage. He often lost control when he was angry but to him, this was a special kind of anger. It was the type of anger that made him want to strangle Celord with his bare hands.

Patrick closed his eyes for a moment. Then, he slowly opened them. A smile spread across his face. A plan was forming in his mind. Yes, he was out for blood. But like the businessman he was, he had to handle business like a businessman would – with a clear mind.

Setting his sights on Celord, he now saw him as a threat that had to be dealt with. This was Celord's and what better person to do the dirty work than the man who caused all the chaos? It was time to settle the score.

"I am heading out to Stoddard's," Patrick calmly said as he exited his office where his secretary stood near the door, the blood drained from her face.

"If you could just clean up that little accident before I come back…" Patrick gestured toward his ransacked office as the secretary made haste of finding a broom and some cloth.

Chapter 5

Celord frowned as he heard the crunching of wheels on the dirt leading up to his home. The distinct sound of a Packard coming close made it very clear that whoever it was, was out on official business. No one would drive a mobile car at this hour without having a dire emergency or a very important point of business to discuss. And since only the wealthy were able to afford motor vehicles, it certainly intrigued Celord to get up from his chair.

He took one last swig from a glass filled with whiskey and walked toward the foyer to greet the uninvited guest. However, as he made it to the front door, it was already open. In the doorway stood none other than Patrick McGill.

"Good evening, Stoddard," Patrick smiled.

With his mind still buzzing with alcohol, Celord tried to repay the kindness by saying, "McGill! If I had known you were doing your rounds, I would have had supper prepared…"

Celord cleared his throat uncomfortably as it was very unlike McGill to visit those he worked with in person. A busy man such as himself usually had patrons doing those tedious tasks.

"Oh, you needn't worry, I won't be staying long," Patrick said calmly and walked past Celord into the house.

Making himself comfortable in the chair Celord was sitting in earlier, Patrick took a sip of the liquid in Celord's glass. Studying the liquid, he swirled it in the glass as if trying to determine where it was manufactured.

"What can I do for you?" Celord asked, wanting to ensure Patrick didn't see how uncomfortable he was becoming.

"I think you are asking the right question, there…" Patrick threatened as he looked over to Celord with daggers in his eyes. "There is something you can do for me…"

Patrick set the glass down on the table in front of him and stood up. He then came to stand close to Celord while talking in a low voice.

"But first, I want to ask you one simple question. And based on your answer, I will determine what exactly it is I want you to do for me," Patrick whispered.

Celord took a step back. It was clear that this was neither a social visit nor a business one. It was a getting-even visit. And although he knew the day would come when he would have to repent his sins, he didn't think it would be this soon.

"What question might that be?" Celord asked as he felt fear taking over.

"Why would you sell the Copper Outlet Claim?" Patrick spat as he pointed a threatening finger toward Celord.

"It is my claim and I can do with it as I please," Celord tried defending himself.

And although he knew the tactic of playing cat and mouse wouldn't work, he had to play for a little more time.

"Your claim?" Celord frowned mockingly. "See, I thought it was our claim... Or have you forgotten our agreement?"

"I meant to make an appointment to see you about that. I didn't want the opportunity to pass us by and that is why I put forth the proposal to a potential buyer. I was going to inform you about it all..."

Celord knew there was no way out of the rut he had just gotten himself into. He was backed into a corner and there was no way out.

"Now, Stoddard," Patrick laughed mockingly, "How do I know if you are not just trying to get rid of me?"

"I won't do such a thing," Celord added. "Please, McGill, you need to believe me. I didn't intend to keep the information from you."

Celord slanted toward begging since he knew what happened to people who dared cross Patrick McGill. He could still remember the screams coming from behind the butcher's shop when McGill caught three of his mining employees walking off with undeclared gold in their pockets.

"There is no need for you to start begging for your life... If you value your life, that is..." Patrick said as he walked over to the sofa once more to sit down.

"The answer to you being alive or not is simple. Get the miners off Copper Outlet. Then sign the claim over to me. Do that successfully and you will live. Fail to do this, and you will die," Patrick explained like he was talking to a child.

'But how... They purchased the claim and paid for it! They are already mining the drift!" Celord couldn't believe what Patrick was asking of him.

That would mean he would need to come clean about his dishonesty. There was no way he was going to let Gordon know the truth. It would cast the entire company in a bad light. He had Gordon in his pocket and could make more than double the amount of profit from the Copper Outlet. But only if Patrick let sleeping dogs lie.

"Stoddard, I know you will do the right thing," Patrick said. "I am giving you a chance to make this right. Get those men away from the drift and give Copper Outlet to me at no cost. I don't care how you do it."

"No cost?" Celord stuttered. "Are you mad!"

With his calm temper suddenly flaring into frustration, Patrick grabbed a cook's knife laying on the counter and lunged at Celord.

Gripping him near the nape of his neck while pointing the knife at his jugular, Patrick seethed, "You will get them off my land and give the claim to me. If you think that you, Stoddard, will overpower me, you are mistaken. I own you and don't you forget that."

Patrick then ordered Celord to put his hand on the counter. "Since you double crossed me I will take your finger. Don't move your hand!" Patrick brought the knife down and Celord's pointer finger fell to the floor in a pool of blood.

"Next time I take your life..."

Patrick let go of Celord's neck, turned around and walked out of the house, leaving the front door wide open. While writhing in pain and almost passing out, Celord grabbed a towel to wrap his hand and stop the bleeding. For what seemed like hours, he dared not move.

He had no choice. He had to obey McGill. If he didn't do as he was told, he would be used as an example to show others what it meant to cross Patrick McGill.

***

Patrick stood on a mound of soil as he looked down onto the miners drifting in and out of the Copper Queen mine in Mayer the following day. Beside him, at the bottom of the mound, stood two well-built men with guns holstered at their sides. Their job was to protect Patrick and since he was a man that was not liked very much, it took a few men at a time to keep him from harm's way. However, to Patrick, it felt like he was the king while his guard and the miners were his servants; working day and night to make him one of the richest men in the New State of Arizona.

"Could I have a word, Sir?" one of the mining bosses glanced up at Patrick and squinted in the sun.

Getting down from the mound, Patrick grunted, "I hope you come bearing good news. I could use some of that today."

"Unfortunately, not, Sir," the mining boss replied while shifting from one foot to the other while eyeing the guards. "We have been mining this drift for a total of four months now. And we are yet to find any sign of natural gold... We have not found any trace of artifacts, let alone Aztec ones."

Patrick slowly turned his head toward the mining boss while deciding if he should let his anger loose on the sorry fool or just let him walk away.

"That's a shame. A very big shame," Patrick said with a sly smile.

The mining boss, accustomed to Patrick's unpredictable behavior, nodded and continued, "I am not sure it would be wise to continue digging at this point in time. Perhaps we should focus on mining a different claim?"

"If I wanted your advice, I would have asked for it," Patrick said. "No, we need to keep digging. Get every single miner inside that drift and keep digging. They'll just have to keep looking."

Knowing better than to argue, the mining boss turned, gave a shrill whistle and motioned with his hands. Following the instruction, all miners outside the mine turned to head back inside. It didn't matter if they were tired, hadn't had anything to eat or drink in hours or felt like the world weighed down on their shoulders. When Patrick McGill's eyes were on them, they did as they were told without hesitating.

After the last head disappeared inside the mine, Patrick turned his attention to his guards, "You know what to do."

The guards nodded, picked up a few wooden crates and started walking down toward the entrance of the mine. Carefully, they placed the crates in the mine and lifted the lids. Inside, blocks of mining dynamite glared back at them.

Calmly, they walked back toward Patrick, who stood at a safe distance.

"Let it rain!" Patrick yelled in an excited voice.

Both guards let go of the fuses they were holding.

At first, there was an eerie silence. And then, suddenly, a blinding flash illuminated the surrounding darkness as a deafening roar tore through the air. The ground rumbled violently, sending shockwaves through everything in its path.

Chunks of rock, dirt and debris were hurled in every direction, propelled by the explosive force of the blast. Flames and smoke billow outwards. The once-stable walls of the mine were instantly reduced to rubble and the very foundations of the earth seemed to shake and groan under the weight of the explosion.

The sound was both terrifying and awe-inspiring, a symphony of destruction that filled the senses and left a lasting impression on all who witnessed it. The air was thick with dust making it difficult to breathe.

As the dust began to settle, the full extent of the damage became apparent. The Copper Queen was unrecognizable, reduced to a mangled heap of wood and rock.

Patrick had just ordered the entire mine, with all the miners inside, to be blown up. Each and every single individual in the mine was buried alive.

"At least I won't be paying wages this week," Patrick commented as he scanned the caved-in area that once was Copper Queen.

With no remorse, he seemed to enjoy the scene in front of him. The guards, obedient and loyal to their boss, stood with blank stares on their faces. After all, it wasn't the first time they had blown up a drift with miners still inside…

Within an hour, word had gotten out of the explosion at the Copper Queen. As the Sherriff and deputies made their way to the mine, it seemed apparent that one would be found alive. However, in an effort to ensure no one might still be alive, they scanned the rubble and called out to anyone who might need medical assistance.

Making their way through over loose rocks and debris scattered everywhere, authorities picked up the remains of abandoned mining equipment. Broken wooden supports and twisted metal track jut out at odd angles, making it look like a death trap.

Patrick, surrounded by his guards, calmly lit a cigar as he watched the Mayor of Prescott, accompanied by the Sherriff head in his direction.

"Such an unfortunate accident," Patrick said as they came to stand next to him.

Without flinching, he handed the Mayor and Sherriff a satchel with each containing a gold bar. Both men peeked into the small satin bags and smiled with satisfaction.

"I agree. Rather unfortunate," the Mayor replied, happy to accept payment for his silence.

"I take it that the correct paperwork will be filled out to render this an accident?" Patrick turned toward the Sherriff.

Nodding, the Sherriff said, "All evidence leads to the conclusion that this occurrence is a mere casualty of mining."

With both the Sherriff and the Mayor in his pocket, it seemed like it was going to be business as usual within a couple of weeks.

He had a treasure to find and needed to get miners willing to go the extra mile.

Chapter 6

Gordon and Chase were deep in the bowels of the Copper Outlet mine drift, when they stumbled upon something unexpected. As they were chipping away at the rock face, they noticed a glint of gold in the dim light of their lanterns. They exchanged a curious look and worked together to chip away at the surrounding rock.

As they uncovered more of the mysterious object, their eyes widened in amazement. Before them was a solid gold Jaguar. The sculpture was intricately detailed, with sharp claws and an intimidating snarl. The two men were stunned. They had never seen anything like it before.

Gordon carefully picked up the statue, feeling its weight in his hands. He turned it over and examined every inch of the impressive work of art. The gold was pure and unblemished, with no visible signs of wear or age. It was like the Jaguar had been waiting there for centuries, to be discovered.

Chase could barely contain his excitement. "Do you know how much this thing is worth?" he exclaimed, staring at the Jaguar in awe.

Gordon nodded, "This is a remarkable piece of history," he said, marveling at the level of craftsmanship. "To the right buyer, it would be worth a pretty penny!"

Gordon and Chase had always dreamed of expanding their mining operation, but they never had the capital to do so. But with the golden Jaguar, they suddenly had the funds they needed to take their operation to the next level.

They knew they needed new mining machines and tools to extract more gold from the mine, but they also knew that the machines and tools they needed were expensive. So, they decided to sell the Jaguar to raise the necessary funds.

Gordon and Chase were both a little nervous as they walked into the Prescott Assay Office, clutching the wrapped-up statue. A rather stout-looking man with wide brim glasses examined the Jaguar with expert eyes, and Gordon and Chase held their breath as they waited for the spot price. Having the precious metal tested was the best way to determine the amount of money they were going to get.

"I would price this artifact at $1653 as gold sells for $20.67 per ounce, since you have about 5 pounds of it right here," the assayer replied.

"I am sure we'd be able to get more if we sell to a collector," Chase mentioned, thoughtfully.

Determined to get commission from this sale, the assayer interjected, "I know of a collector who would definitely be interested in what you have here and would be willing to pay more. If you come back in two days, I am sure you'd get a good price from him as well."

The original quote was more than they could have ever imagined. Gordon and Chase exchanged looks, and after a brief moment of hesitation, they agreed to return to meet with the collector.

Two days later, as discussed, Gordon and Chase, filled with anxious anticipation, returned to the Assay Office to have the collector inspect the Jaguar.

While making their way through main street in Mayer, towards Prescott, Gordon noticed that they were being followed by two masked men on horseback. It was clear that these men knew Gordon and Chase were carrying something of high value.

Not wanting the thieves to catch them off-guard and potentially have the chance of getting them off their horses, Gordon and Chase had to think fast.

Gordon looked at Chase as they rode side by side. The masked men were advancing quite quickly. Gordon nodded toward Chase, giving him a silent signal as to what he needed to do. Suddenly, Chase took off on his horse, running like the wind. Both thieves set off after their target, guessing that Chase was the one with the artefact in his possession.

Focusing on the task at hand, Gordon pulled his gun from its holster and shot one of them. Chase then doubled back and took aim at the other, hitting the last robber square on the forehead.

With both thieves taken out, their horses continued to gallop frantically with the dead bodies flopping over the saddles.

"Are you alright?" Gordon gasped as he trotted over to his son.

"I'm alright. We need to get off the road fast. It's not safe," Chase replied while adrenaline rushed through his veins.

At the Assay office, Gordon and Chase made sure they were not followed by anyone else before entering the building. Both men were very cautious and ready for anything, knowing that the assayer could have tipped the thieves off. As they entered the office, the Assayer seemed a little surprised to see them.

In the Assayer's office, they were introduced to the collector. The collector seemed really anxious and excited when Gordon pulled the solid gold jaguar from his leather side bag.

Trying to calm himself the collector said, "It looks like you two have stumbled across a very old Aztec treasure. The jaguar is a sacred animal that symbolized strength, speed, power and intelligence to the Aztec people. This artifact must have been used by Montezuma himself as a talisman to control his people! Where did you find this?"

Gordon spoke up and said, "Don't worry about that. We are just interested in a price on this object that is greater than the spot price of gold."

With that, the collector said, "I give you $1653 in cash and 10 ounces of gold right now."

Satisfied with the outcome, Gordon agreed to the price. The collector handed a bag full of money and gold to Gordon. Chase counted the money then Gordon handed the gold jaguar over.

With the money from the sale of the Aztec jaguar, Gordon and Chase were able to purchase brand new mining equipment and tools. They spent days researching the best equipment, trying to make sure that every penny was spent wisely.

First on their list were ore carts and track. They wanted a system that could help them extract and move the ore from the mine more efficiently. With a couple new hydraulic drills and a steam-powered compressor, Gordon and Chase felt exhilarated to say the very least.

Next, they focused on tools for the miners. They knew that having the right tools was crucial for safety and productivity. They purchased new helmets and safety gear for their employees, as well as pickaxes and shovels. They also invested in new lanterns that would make it easier for the miners to work deep in the mine.

Finally, Gordon and Chase decided to purchase two colt peacemaker revolvers for protection. While they had never encountered any danger in the mine before, they knew that their newfound success could attract unwanted attention. The revolvers gave them a sense of security and allowed them to focus on their work without worrying about outside threats.

With their new equipment and tools ready to operate on Copper Outlet, Gordon and Chase were eager to put their equipment to work and within 6 months, with a total of 10 new miners added to the team, productivity was at its peak.

While trying to ignore the fact that rumors were spread around Prescott and Mayer of Gordon and Chase having discovered a potential treasure chest of valuable items in their mine, Copper Outlet opened its crevices to reveal its true potential.

***

The sound of picks striking rock echoed through the dark mine as Gordon and Chase worked side by side. They had been mining for hours, hoping to find something more. The Jaguar had set the stakes high.

Suddenly, Chase's pick struck something hard. "Dad, I think I found something!" he shouted.

Gordon hurried over to his son's side and peered into the small crevice that he had been working on. Sure enough, there was something glinting in the rock.

"What is it?" Gordon asked.

Chase pulled at the strange object, uncovering a dirt-covered object, "It looks like a mask of some sort. Has to be very old, by the looks of it…"

Gordon held his breath as he realized what he was looking at. And in all his years of mining, he would have never thought he would ever lay eyes on something as valuable as this. Yes, he had heard of this object being hidden somewhere in Arizona or Utah but for the most part, he thought it was purely old-wives' tales. Yet, in his son's hands lay an Aztec mask and with intricate details adorning the piece, it appeared to be Montezuma's Mask!

Montezuma's Mask was a stunning work of art and a true testament to the craftsmanship of the ancient Aztec civilization. The mask was made of pure gold and adorned with precious stones, including emeralds, rubies and sapphires.

Designed in a traditional Aztec style, it had intricate patterns and symbols that represented various aspects of Aztec culture and mythology. The front of the mask was adorned with a large sun disk, which was surrounded by symbols that represented the sun, the moon and the stars.

The mask also had two large, circular eye holes that were decorated with emeralds, giving the impression that the mask was staring directly at the viewer. The nose of the mask was short and pointed, with delicate lines and curves that created a sense of movement and flow.

The mouth of the mask was left open, revealing a set of perfect, gleaming teeth made of ivory. The lips were carved with a delicate curve that gave the impression of a slight smile and the edges of the mask were adorned with metal feathers. The feathers themselves were made of a variety of materials, including gold, silver, and precious gems.

After what seemed like hours, Gordon and Chase tear their eyes away from the ancient treasure.

"How did it get here?" Chase managed to say.

"This mask must be connected to the bones we uncovered in the chamber nearby." Gordon replied as he made a few calculations in a small leather notebook he always kept in his pocket.

If his theory was correct, they had just discovered a treasure that was hidden all the way back in the 16th century!

In the early 16th century, the Aztec Empire was one of the wealthiest and most powerful civilizations in the world. The empire's riches came from its vast reserves of gold, silver, and other precious metals, which were mined from the mountains of central Mexico.

But in 1519, the Aztecs' fortunes took a dark turn when the Spanish conquistador Hernan Cortes arrived in Mexico with a small army of soldiers. Cortes had come to conquer the Aztecs and claim their riches for Spain, and he was determined to succeed.

When Montezuma II, the Aztec emperor, heard of Cortes' arrival, he knew that his empire was in grave danger. He knew from his previous meeting with Cortes that the Spanish conquistadores wanted to take over his empire and plunder the Aztec Empire treasure.

Montezuma II knew that the Spanish would stop at nothing to get their hands on the Aztec Empire's gold. So, he came up with a plan to protect the empire's most valuable treasures. He ordered 500 of his bravest and most trusted soldiers to take the empire's gold and transport it north, away from the Spanish invaders.

The soldiers were given strict orders to keep the location of the gold a secret and to dig mines or find caves to hide it. They were told to stay away from the major trade routes and to travel only at night to avoid detection. The soldiers knew that their mission was of the utmost importance, and they were determined to succeed.

For months, the soldiers traveled through the mountains and valleys of central Mexico, carrying the empire's gold with them. They faced many challenges along the way, including harsh weather, rugged terrain, and attacks by bandits and rival tribes.

But despite these obstacles, the soldiers persevered. They dug deep into the earth, creating secret tunnels and chambers to hide the gold. They covered the entrances with rocks and dirt, disguising them as natural formations to avoid detection.

However, according to legend, a huge cave-in caused many of the Aztecs to be buried alive along with the treasure. Forgotten to the world.

"Until now," Gordon said aloud as he smiled at his son.

Patrick stormed into Celord's office; his face contorted with anger.

"What's this I hear about my claim, Celord?" he barked, throwing a piece of paper from his informant into Celord's desk. "It appears that someone found a solid gold Aztec Jaguar worth a fortune in the Copper Outlet. And where was I? Oh, that's right! You sold my claim out from under me, you fool!"

Celord swallowed hard, knowing he was in deep trouble. However, the fact that treasure was found at the mining claim intrigued him.

"An Aztec Jaguar?" Celord frowned, trying to imagine how much something like that would be worth.

"Montezuma's Jaguar!" Patrick spat. "And now not only is my mine in the grubby hands of some miner trying to strike it rich but my treasure has gone with it!"

Patrick had a reputation for being a cruel and ruthless man, and Celord, for the second time, knew that he had crossed him. As he rubbed the bandage surrounding his now-missing finger, he knew he was backed into a corner.

Over the past couple of days, Celord had tried to avoid Patrick, Gordon and Chase but it seemed like life was catching up to him faster than he could run. He tried to reason with Patrick.

"Patrick, I didn't know about the treasure. You can't blame me for what the miners found. I am working on getting the claim back, I swear..."

Patrick slammed his fist onto the desk, making Celord jump.

"Don't you dare tell me what I can and can't do, Celord. You made a big mistake crossing me. Now, I want my claim back with the treasure, do you hear me?"

Celord's heart sank as he realized what Patrick was suggesting.

"You want me to torture the miners to give it back? I won't do it, Patrick. I won't be a part of your sick games."

Patrick's eyes narrowed, and he leaned in close to Celord.

"You don't have a choice, Celord. Either you help me get my claim back, or you suffer the consequences. And believe me, they won't be pretty."

Celord knew he was trapped. He couldn't go to the authorities, and he couldn't take on Patrick alone. Deep down, he knew that he was about to unleash a monster.

Chapter 7

Gordon and Chase had just finished a long day of work at their mine and were walking back to their camp when they heard a loud crack of thunder followed by a blinding light surrounding the area. They looked up at the sky, wondering if a storm was approaching, but the sky was still clear.

"What trickery is this?" Gordon said as he stood still, trying to figure out what just happened.

Suddenly, a bolt of lightning streaked across the sky and hit a nearby hill, causing a small rockslide. Startled by the strange occurrence, Chase stumbled to the ground as the earth shook beneath their feet.

As they regained their footing, they heard the panicked whinny of a horse. Following the sounds of distress, they came across one of the horses used to haul rocks. It had been struck by the lightning bolt. With its limbs weak, a scorching wound running all the way from its chest to its left hoof. The smell of burnt flesh made Chase squirm.

Gordon bent over the severely injured horse, trying to calm it down, but he knew it was too late. The animal had been badly hurt and it was clear that it wasn't going to make it.

He looked concerned. "We have to do something," he said, his voice tense. "We can't just let it suffer."

Chase nodded in agreement, his eyes fixed on the horse. He knew that they had to put the animal out of its misery, but he couldn't bring himself to do it.

Gordon told Chase to get his pistol. Chase ran to his tent cabin and grabbed his loaded Colt peacemaker. Gordon took the pistol and with a quick motion, he shot the animal in the head, and it fell to the ground, motionless.

Chase looked away, feeling sick to his stomach. He couldn't believe that this had happened. It was just another reminder of how dangerous their work was.

Gordon put a hand on his son's shoulder, trying to offer some comfort. "We'll be more careful from now on," he said, his voice low. "We'll make sure everyone stays safe."

After a few hours working the dirt in Copper Outlet, Chase eased up a little as he worked alongside one of the miners near the new shaker box.

The sound of the shaker box echoed as they worked to sift through the gravel for any signs of gold. They had not been working that long but Chase could feel that his hands were sore and calloused.

Suddenly, there was a loud thump, and the miner next to him cried out in pain. His hand had become stuck in the shaker box, and he couldn't pull it out. Writhing in pain with blood dripping onto the dirt, the machine grinded to a halt as it settled on splinters of bone and flesh.

"Help!" the miner yelled, staring at Chase in pure panic. "I'm stuck!"

Gordon, who heard the cry for help, rushed over to see what had happened. He gasped as he saw the miner's hand trapped in the shaker box. He immediately knew that the miner wouldn't be able to leave the mine with his hand intact.

He put his hand on the miner's shoulder while trying to stay calm. While giving a few orders to the crowd of miners who came to help, it was decided that the miner would need to have his hand amputated.

"Does anyone have some whiskey? Water? And an axe? He won't make it out alive if we don't act fast! This man will die in the next minute if we don't cut him loose! Go and fetch the doctor! Bring the doctor, hurry!" Gordon commanded.

"I can't do this!" the miner screamed in pain as he realized what was about to happen. He could feel the life draining from his wrists and over the machine.

With two miners holding him steady, another miner poured whiskey onto the wound and gestured for the injured man to take a swig for the pain. Then, with a sickening thud, Gordon bought a sharp axe down onto the miner's arm, cutting him free from the machine.

Falling to the dirt, the miner's anguished echoes suddenly fell silent. His eyes glazed over as his breathing stopped. It was too late. The miner had succumbed to his injuries.

Chase cursed under his breath, feeling sick to his stomach. Ever since they had discovered the Aztec mask, strange things had been happening in the mine. Tools would go missing, tunnels would cave in unexpectedly, and now one of their own had been injured. The mask was cursed, he was sure of it.

Hours later, when the horror of the accident caused the mine to shut down for the rest of the day, Gordon sat down on a crate with his hands in his hair.

Chase sat down next to him, a worried look etched on his face. "Do you ever get the feeling that the mine is cursed?" he asked, his voice low.

Gordon looked at his son, understanding the weight of his words. "I know what you mean," he said with a sigh. "It's been one thing after another since we found that mask."

Chase nodded in agreement. "I feel like someone's out to get us," he said, looking around the mine as if someone was watching them.

Gordon put a comforting hand on his son's shoulder. "We've been in this business for a long time," he said. "We know that accidents happen. It's just that this time, it all feels different."

Chase shook his head. "I don't think it's just accidents," he said. "Something is sabotaging us. And I think it has something to do with that mask."

Gordon frowned, deep in thought. He didn't want to believe that someone was sabotaging their mine, but he couldn't shake the feeling that his son was right.

"We'll have to keep a close eye on everything from now on," he said, his voice firm. "We can't let anything else happen to our miners or our mine."

***

Gordon sat quietly in his armchair, staring at the beautiful, ornate Aztec mask resting on the coffee table in front of him. His son paced back and forth behind him, restless and anxious.

"We can't keep it," Chase said, stopping behind his father's chair. "It's cursed, or haunted, or something. Every time we find something valuable, someone gets hurt."

Gordon sighed heavily, rubbing his forehead. "I know, son. I've been thinking about it too. But we can't just sell it like any other piece of gold or silver. This is different. If we sell it, everyone will know what we've found. And then what? Claim jumpers, thieves, con artists... they'll all be after us."

Chase scowled. "But what other choice do we have? We can't just keep it here, taunting us. We need to get rid of it."

Gordon leaned back in his chair, staring up at his son. "I know, I know. I agree with you. We need to sell it. But we have to be careful. We can't let anyone know what it is or where it came from. We need to find a buyer we can trust."

Chase nodded, relief flooding over him. "Okay, that's a start. We'll find someone we can trust. And then we'll get rid of this damn thing once and for all."

Gordon reached out and patted his son's hand. "We'll figure it out, son. We always do."

That evening Gordon and Chase sat across from each other at the Mayer Saloon. They both had sweat on their foreheads from working in the mines all day, but they had more pressing matters to attend to.

"Gordon, we need to be discreet," Chase said, taking a swig of his whiskey.

"I know, Chase," Gordon replied, wiping his forehead with a handkerchief. "We can't let anyone know about the mask."

Ever since they discovered the Aztec mask in their mining claim, the mine had been plagued with accidents and bad luck. They knew they needed to sell it or auction it off, but they also knew that they couldn't risk drawing attention to themselves.

"We need to take the mask to auction in New York," Gordon said, leaning in closer to Chase. "There are some wealthy collectors there who would pay top dollar for something like this."

Chase nodded in agreement. "But we have to be careful. We don't want to attract any unwanted attention."

Gordon finished his whiskey and stood up. "I'll start making the arrangements for the trip. We'll leave as soon as possible."

Chase nodded, watching as Gordon made his way out of the saloon. He couldn't shake the feeling that they were playing with fire, but they had no other choice. They needed to get rid of the cursed mask before it destroyed their mine and their livelihood.

***

Gordon and Chase rode their horses South out of camp through Mayer. By the following afternoon, leaving the dust and noise behind. The sun was just beginning to set, casting a warm golden glow across the landscape.

As they rode, they passed through vast stretches of land, dotted with cacti and sparse vegetation. The hot desert air was thick and oppressive, and they could feel beads of sweat forming on their foreheads. Gordon adjusted his wide-brimmed hat and pulled up the collar of his leather jacket to shield himself from the sun.

Chase rode beside him, his eyes scanning the horizon for any signs of danger. He carried a loaded revolver at his side, a precaution they had both agreed upon before setting out on their journey.

As the sun began to dip below the horizon, the sky transformed into a fiery blaze of reds and oranges. Gordon and Chase rode on, their horses galloping across the dusty terrain. The rhythmic sound of their horses' hooves echoed through the silence of the desert, a steady beat that seemed to carry them forward.

While providing their horses with a well-deserved break, Gordon untied the large leather messenger bag they had brought with them and placed it on the ground beside one of the horses. The bag was thick, padded leather, with brass hardware and leather straps.

Gordon knelt down and unlatched the top bag flap, revealing the inside. The interior was lined with soft velvet. In the center of the bag lay the Aztec mask, carefully wrapped in a silk cloth.

Coming to stand next to his father, Chase lifted the mask out of the messenger bag and examined it closely. "This thing gives me the creeps," he said, shuddering slightly.

Gordon nodded in agreement. "We need to make sure it stays hidden until we find a buyer."

They carefully wrapped the mask back up and placed it back in the bag. They then locked the bag and secured it with additional leather straps.

"We should keep the key with us at all times," Chase said, tucking the key into his pocket.

While they made camp for the evening, they were up before dawn the next morning to make their way to the Southern Pacific Railroad Depot in Tucson that would carry them to New York.

***

As Gordon and Chase arrived at the bustling train station, the sound of steam engines hissing and whistling filled the air.

They led their horses to a nearby stable and handed them over to the stable hand. Gordon gave the man some coins and instructed him to take good care of the animals.

With their horses taken care of, Gordon and Chase turned their attention to the messenger bag that held the cursed mask. Gordon threw the heavy mask, bag onto his shoulder. Chase grabbed their other bag that held their clothes and weapons.

The train whistle blew, signaling that it was time to board. Gordon and Chase made their way to the platform. The train was long and sleek, with rows of passenger cars stretching as far as the eye could see.

As they boarded the train, they were relieved to find that they had a private compartment to themselves. They carefully set their bags on the luggage rack above their seats, and then settled in for the long journey ahead.

Gordon and Chase kept a watchful eye on the bag, never letting it out of their sight. They knew that they had a valuable treasure in their possession, one that could change their lives forever. But they also knew that it was a dangerous thing to have, one that could bring them harm if it fell into the wrong hands.

To pass the time, Gordon sat poring over a thick, leather-bound book he had purchased at a local shop in Prescott. The book was old and worn, with yellowed pages and faded ink, but it contained a wealth of information about Aztec treasure.

He carefully turned the pages, his fingers tracing the faded lines of text. He had always been fascinated by the Aztec culture, with their elaborate temples and treasures, and he had hoped that this book would shed some light on the mysterious mask they had uncovered in their mine.

As he read, he discovered that the Aztecs were known for their vast wealth, with treasures made of gold, silver, and precious stones. They believed that their gods demanded offerings of treasure and human sacrifice, and so they created elaborate objects and sculptures to appease them.

Gordon's eyes widened as he read about the famous Aztec Sun Stone, a massive, intricately carved disk of stone that was said to have been used as a calendar. He also learned about the Aztec treasure hoard that the Spanish conquistadors had plundered, taking thousands of pounds of gold and silver back to Europe.

But it was the section on Aztec masks that caught Gordon's attention. He read about the masks that the Aztecs had worn during their religious ceremonies, some of them made of gold or jade, with intricate carvings and precious stones.

He came to the conclusion that the curse was not a simple superstition, but rather a real and powerful force that had been unleashed when they had uncovered the mask.

As he studied the intricate carvings of an image of the mask in the book, he couldn't help but feel a sense of unease. The figures depicted on the mask were twisted and grotesque, with jagged teeth and bony claws. It was clear to Gordon that this was not a benign artifact, but rather a powerful talisman with the ability to inflict harm.

He thought back to the accidents that had plagued their mine ever since they had uncovered the mask. The collapses, the injuries, the deaths. It all seemed so clear to him now. The mask was cursed, and they had to get rid of it before any more harm could be done.

But as he thought about how to dispose of the mask, he couldn't help but wonder about the ancient Aztec culture that had created it. What had they intended the mask to be used for? Was it meant to be a weapon, or a symbol of power?

Gordon shook his head, pushing those thoughts aside. He knew that he couldn't get too caught up in the mask's history or its potential value. He had to focus on the present, on getting rid of it and keeping himself and Chase safe. Now all he and Chase had to do was settle in and ride the train for 80 hours.

Chapter 8

Following the first 50 hours on the train, Gordon and Chase settled into their seats, enjoying the rhythmic sound of the train wheels on the tracks. The train was a marvel of engineering, traveling across vast distances at incredible speeds.

As they relaxed, a man wearing a frock with a white collar and a camera around his neck, entered their designated seating area. He was of average height, with a clean-shaven face and piercing blue eyes. His refined mannerisms hinted at a certain level of sophistication. The man approached Gordon and Chase, introducing himself as Father Browne. In a polite voice, Gordon welcomed the Father to sit with them.

"So, Father where is your flock?" Gordon asked.

Father Browne explained, "I have no flock, I am a Jesuit sent by the Pope, on a very important mission!"

Chase exclaimed, "You personally know the Pope?"

"Yes, I do." Father Browne said.

Father Browne looked at the locked messenger bag and questioned, "So it looks like you two are on an important trip, also? You must be transporting something of value."

Gordon and Chase exchanged a quick glance, then Gordon speaks. "No, just personal items."

The man nodded, seeming to understand. "I see. Well, I'm sorry to pry. It's just that I'm a bit of a collector myself, and I'm always on the lookout for interesting artifacts."

Gordon and Chase were curious about the Father's interest in rare artifacts, and they engaged him in conversation. The priest was enthusiastic about the Churches' collection and shared his knowledge of ancient religious artifacts, like statues, masks, and ritual objects. He talked about the symbolism and cultural significance of these items and how they had been used throughout history.

"Some of the ancient religious artifacts are dangerous with destructive powers." Father Browne explained. "Certain items needed to be locked up, in deep underground tombs, for safe keeping!"

As the conversation continued, Gordon and Chase grew more and more intrigued by the Father's knowledge and passion for rare artifacts. They shared stories of their own travels and their mining operation back in Arizona.

Despite their initial hesitations, Gordon and Chase found themselves warming up to the Priest. They sensed that he was genuine in his interest of artifacts and that he respected their privacy regarding the contents of their locked bag.

However, as they talked, the man's eyes kept flicking towards the messenger bag. Gordon and Chase noticed his interest and exchanged another quick glance.

Father Browne kept staring at the messenger bag, his hands twitching with anticipation. "You say it's just personal items, but I have a feeling there's more to it than that," he said, his voice low and menacing. "I must insist that you open it so that I can see for myself."

Gordon and Chase were taken aback by the man's sudden change in demeanor. They had enjoyed talking with him, but now they felt uneasy.

Gordon spoke up, his voice firm. "I'm sorry, Father, but we can't open the bag."

Father Browne's face twisted in anger as he glared at Chase and Gordon. His eyes flicked towards the bag, and he licked his lips hungrily. "You will open that trunk now, or I will be forced to take matters into my own hands," he snarled, his voice low and menacing.

Gordon stepped forward; his fists clenched at his sides. He towered over the Jesuit, his broad shoulders blocking the man's view of the locked messenger bag. "I think it's time for you to leave our train car," he said, his voice cold and hard.

But the Jesuit wasn't backing down. He was a man used to getting what he wanted, and he wouldn't be deterred by a couple of amateurs like Chase and Gordon. "I'm not leaving until I see what's inside that locked bag," he said, his eyes flashing with fury.

Chase and Gordon knew they had to act fast. They couldn't risk losing the bag or the treasure it contained. They exchanged a quick glance, silently communicating their plan. "We're not going to open the bag," Chase said firmly. "If you don't leave now, we'll have to call the authorities."

Father Browne, laughed bitterly, his eyes glinting with malice. "I doubt they'll be able to help you," he sneered. "You two are in way over your heads."

Gordon had had enough. Without warning, he lunged forward and punched the Jesuit in the nose. The man stumbled backwards, clutching his bleeding nose. Gordon attempts to throw another punch but the Jesuit blocks it with his left hand.

The Jesuit wasn't so easily deterred. He regained his footing and lunged towards the bag, determined to get his hands on the treasure inside. Chase and Gordon knew they had to act fast to stop him.

They grabbed the bag and lifted it up, moving it out of the Jesuit's reach. But the man was persistent. He kept coming at them, his fists clenched and his eyes wild as if he was in some sort of trance.

Chase and Gordon knew they had to get out of the train car before things got even more out of hand. They quickly gathered their things and left the train car, not looking back. They knew they had to get as far away from the Jesuit as possible or risk being caught in his grasp.

As they moved through the train cars, they could feel the weight of the danger they were in. Father Browne, had made it clear that he was willing to do whatever it takes to get his hands on the bag and the treasure it held. They had no idea how they were going to get out of this mess, but they knew they had to act fast.

Suddenly, they heard the sound of footsteps behind them. They turned around to see the Jesuit, his face contorted in rage, hot on their heels. "You two can't run forever!" he shouted. "You have crossed the Catholic Church."

Chase and Gordon quickened their pace, trying to put as much distance between themselves and the Jesuit as possible. But it soon became clear that they weren't going to be able to outrun him forever. They needed a plan, and fast.

As they reached the next car, they heard a voice behind them. "Looking for someone?" The voice belonged to a tall, muscular man in a suit, with a stern expression on his face. I am a federal agent." The man explained. He flashes his BI (Bureau of Investigation) badge.

Gordon and Chase exchanged a surprised glance, "Actually, yes," Gordon said. "We had an altercation with the Jesuit Priest in the last car. He tried to steal one of our bags."

The BI Agent's expression hardened. "I think I know who you are talking about?" "We have been investigating certain crimes that have been linked to the Jesuits".

The BI Agent cracked his knuckles. "Leave it to me. I'll take care of him."

Gordon and Chase exchanged a surprised look. They had expected the Agent to be busy with his own assignment, but he seemed more than willing to help them. "Are you sure?" Chase asked. "We don't want to get you in trouble."

The Agent nodded his head. "Don't worry about it. It's my job to keep the train safe from threats like this."

With that, the Agent took off towards the back of the train, his footsteps echoing through the narrow corridors. Gordon and Chase followed close behind, eager to see what he would do.

As they reached the last car, they could see the Jesuit nursing his injury, in his seat. He looked up as they approached, a smirk on his face. "Back again, boys?"

The BI Agent stepped forward; his eyes cold. "I'm afraid you need to leave these men alone," he said. "You're causing a disturbance on this train, and I can't have that."

The Jesuit laughed. "I haven't done anything wrong," he said. "I was just trying to have a conversation with these two. They got violent, not me."

Gordon and Chase exchanged a glance. They knew that the Jesuit was lying, but they couldn't prove it.

The BI Agent wasn't convinced either. "I think you're lying," he said, his voice low. "I think you're trying to steal something from the men?"

The Jesuit's expression turned to one of anger. "How dare you accuse me of such a thing!" he said. "I demand that you leave me alone."

The BI Agent's eyes hardened. "I'm afraid I can't do that," he said, taking a step forward. "I'm going to have to ask you to leave the train at the next station."

The Jesuit stood up; his fists clenched. "I'm not going anywhere," he said. "I demand that you leave me alone!"

The BI Agent stepped forward to confront the Jesuit, his stance confident and self-assured. The Jesuit glared at him with hatred in his eyes, his fists clenched and ready to strike. For a moment, there was a tense silence as the two men faced off against each other.

Then, with lightning-fast reflexes, the Jesuit launched himself at the BI Agent, throwing a wild punch at his head. The Agent dodged the blow, sidestepping to the left and countering with a hard punch of his own.

The Jesuit stumbled backwards, but he was quick to recover, coming back with a flurry of punches that the Agent blocked and parried with ease. He was clearly experienced in hand-to-hand combat, and his movements were precise and calculated.

The Bureau Agent responded with a swift kick to the Jesuit's midsection, knocking him off-balance and giving him an opening to launch a devastating uppercut. The blow landed squarely on the Jesuit's jaw, sending him reeling backwards with a look of shock on his face.

For a moment, the Jesuit seemed dazed and disoriented, but then he regained his composure and launched himself at Agent once again. The two men grappled and struggled, each trying to gain the upper hand.

It was a fierce battle, with neither man giving an inch. Punches were exchanged, kicks were thrown, and the sound of flesh hitting flesh echoed through the train car.

Finally, the Agent managed to get the Jesuit in a headlock, squeezing his arm tightly around the Jesuit's neck. The Jesuit struggled and thrashed, but he was no match for the BI Agent's strength and skills.

With a final twist of his arm, the Agent brought the Jesuit to the ground, pinning him there with a knee to the back. The Jesuit let out a cry of pain and frustration, his struggles weakening as he realized he was defeated.

Gordon and Chase watched in amazement as the Agent subdued the Jesuit, impressed by his skill and determination. It was clear that he was not just any BI Agent, but someone who had undergone extensive training in hand to hand, combat and self-defense.

After the Agent had subdued the Jesuit, he sat him up against the train car and began questioning him. Gordon and Chase exchanged bewildered glances as the Jesuit revealed that he had been sent by the Pope to retrieve the mask.

"The Pope?" Gordon repeated incredulously.

"Yes, he received word of your discovery and wanted the mask for himself," the Jesuit confirmed.

Chase interjected, "But why would the Pope want the mask?"

"I don't know," the Jesuit admitted. "But he made it clear that it was a matter of utmost importance."

The BI Agent scoffed, "Well, it looks like he sent the wrong guy. Now, what should we do with you?"

The Jesuit hung his head and expressed remorse, "I understand the gravity of what I have done. I accept my punishment."

Gordon and Chase felt torn. They were grateful that the Jesuit had come clean, but they were unsure about what to do next. They wondered if there were others who knew about the mask.

"Did anyone else know about the mask?" Gordon asked.

"As far as I know, I was the only one sent to retrieve it," the Jesuit replied, shaking his head.

Chase was skeptical, "How can we be sure?"

The Jesuit shrugged, "I can only speak for myself. But I assure you, I was the only one sent by the Pope."

Gordon and Chase pondered for a moment before coming to a decision. They had no other choice but to believe the Jesuit.

The BI Agent, without saying a word, dragged the Jesuit to the end of the train car and threw him off the moving train. Gordon and Chase watched in shock as the Jesuit's body tumbled down the embankment and out of sight.

Gordon broke the silence, "How did the Pope even know about the mask?"

Chase added, "And since he knew, did anyone else know?"

He Agent stood before Gordon and Chase, wiping his hands with a white cloth. The man before them appeared different, transformed with a new intensity in his eyes. Something about him had changed, and the duo couldn't quite place what it was.

The Agent's voice was low and menacing as he spoke. "You two possess something that the Bureau of Investigation wants. The Aztec mask you have there in your messenger bag," he said.

Gordon and Chase exchanged a cautious glance. How did The Bureau of Investigation know what mask they had in their possession? The Jesuit had never mentioned the exact details of the mask in question.

"Why should we do that?" Chase demanded.

"Because I can keep you both safe," The Agent replied, his tone persuasive. "I can protect you from whoever else is after that mask. And believe me, there are plenty of people who would kill to get their hands on it."

Gordon and Chase shared another apprehensive look. They knew the Agent was right. They had already survived one attack, and they were convinced that more would follow. However, they weren't prepared to relinquish the mask to a stranger, regardless of how menacing he appeared or who he worked for. His true intentions were after the fact that he had just killed a Jesuit Priest.

"We are capable of defending ourselves," Gordon said resolutely. "We don't need your assistance."

The BI Agent chuckled, and the sound sent shivers down their spines. "Is that so?" he retorted. "You two barely escaped the previous attack. How do you think you'll manage against the next one?"

"We will manage," Chase said, trying to sound confident.

The Bureau Agent shook his head. "I don't think you understand the gravity of the situation. That mask is priceless, and there are people out there who will do whatever it takes to get their hands on it, including killing both of you."

Gordon and Chase exchanged another anxious look. They understood that G-Man was right. They were out of their depth in a world of treachery and greed. They had stumbled upon something priceless, and now they were embroiled in something much bigger than they had ever imagined.

"What do you suggest we do?" Gordon asked, his voice betraying his resignation.

The Agent's smile was sinister, "It's simple," he said. "You give me the mask, and I'll guarantee that you both live to see another day."

Gordon and Chase pondered their options. They knew if they gave up the mask, they would never see a penny from it. They also knew they needed to sell the mask to keep their mining operation afloat. They were uncertain if they could manage it without help. They were uncertain if they could trust the Agent, but they were out of alternatives.

The BI Agent was in the middle of his demand when a loud bang interrupted him. The sound of a gunshot echoed through the train car,

As the Agent fell lifeless on the ground, the train car was filled with the deafening sound of silence. The unexpected gunshot had sent Gordon and Chase into a state of panic, as they quickly took cover behind the closes train seat. Their thoughts were racing as they tried to figure out their next move.

Suddenly, a Cowboy entered the train car with a sly smile on his face. His cold eyes darted towards the BI Agents body and then towards Gordon and Chase, who were frozen with fear.

"Patrick McGill wouldn't want the mask in the hands of some filthy government agent," the Cowboy said with a chuckle. "And he certainly wouldn't want it in the hands of a couple of nobodies like you two."

"Patrick McGill..." Gordon breathed.

Gordon and Chase stared at the scene in utter horror as they tried to piece together what had just happened. The BI Agent, the man who had just saved their lives, now lay on the ground bleeding out. The Cowboy who had just shot him was now pointing his gun directly at them, a sly grin on his face.

As the realization of what had happened set in, Gordon and Chase couldn't believe their own naivety. It all made sense now. Patrick McGill had been on their trail since they had discovered the ancient mask. He must have known about their discovery and sent his goons to retrieve it.

The weight of their situation hit them like a ton of bricks. They were now in the middle of a life and death struggle with a ruthless criminal and his hired gun. And worse yet, they were in possession of something that Patrick would stop at nothing to get his hands on.

Gordon and Chase knew they were in a dangerous situation. The Cowboy's gun was pointed straight at them, and they knew that any sudden movements could result in their deaths. They looked at each other, exchanging a quick glance, silently communicating their fear and uncertainty.

As the Cowboy approached them, his laughter continued. "You know," he said, "I've been tracking you two since you left Mayer."

Gordon and Chase were stunned. They had heard of the Mask's value before, but they never imagined that someone would be willing to kill for it. The Cowboy's cold demeanor made it clear that he was not afraid to do whatever it takes to get his hands on it.

The Cowboy stopped a few feet away from them and lowered his gun. "So, what's it going be?" he asked with a smirk. "Are you going to hand over the Mask, or am I going to take it from you?"

Gordon and Chase hesitated, knowing that they couldn't just hand over the Mask. They had come too far and risked too much to give it up now. But they also knew that they couldn't fight the Cowboy. He was too well-armed, too experienced, and too dangerous.

After a moment of silence, Gordon finally spoke up. "We don't have the Mask," he said, his voice trembling. "We don't know where it is."

The Cowboy's smirk turned into a scowl. "Don't play games with me," he growled. "I know you have it. And if you don't give it to me, you'll regret it."

In pure hopelessness, Chase shoved the cowboy with all his might, sending him tumbling over the train car seats. The fall causes the Cowboy's gun to discharge. The noise was deafening. Having just enough time to grab the bag, Gordon and Chase ran into the corridor, their eyes wide with fear.

Everyone on this train was a suspect. It was as clear as day. No one was to be trusted.

Gordon and Chase knew they had to act quickly. The cowboy was hot on their heels, and they had to find a way to escape. They ran down the narrow corridors of the steam-powered train, their footsteps echoing through the metal walls. Their hearts were pounding in their chests, and sweat dripped down their foreheads.

The two ran through a populated train car. They then ran towards a baggage car near the front of the train. As they were about to enter the baggage car, a train conductor yells at them.

"Stop, you can't go in there." Gordon explained. "This is an emergency, there is a man trying to kill and rob us. Please let us hide with the baggage. Here is a solid gold Indian Head coin."

The Conductor took the gold coin then let the two into the baggage car and then locked the baggage car door.

They found themselves surrounded with freight, crates and barrels and could hear the cowboy's footsteps growing louder, and they knew they had to hide. Crawling behind one of the large crates, they could hear yelling and fighting outside the door. Realizing they needed to move, Chase pointed out a hatch in the ceiling.

They pushed aside the crates and climbed up to the hatch, pushed it open and hoisted themselves up onto the roof of the train. The wind whipped past them, and they could feel the train speeding along the tracks. Running along the roof, their feet slipped on the metal surface as they jumped over a gap in the roof and landed on the next car.

As they ran, they could hear the cowboy shouting curses behind them. They knew they had to find a way to lose him.

Spotting a hatch on the roof of the next car, they made a run for it, pushed it open and climbed inside. Finding themselves in a sleeping car with doors lining both sides of the walk way, they could hear the cowboy's footsteps on the roof above them, and they knew he was getting closer.

Running down the corridor, they tried each door as they went. One of the doors opened, and they stumbled inside. It was an empty bunk room. They heard some yelling outside the door. It sounds as if the Cowboy has disturbed and angered a few passengers. Finally, the commotion died down, and they knew they had lost him.

As they lay there, they realized that they had been forced to confront their own fears and weaknesses. They knew that they could never let their guard down, and that they had to be ready for anything if they wanted to survive.

They had managed to outsmart him for now, but they still had a long way to go before they could feel safe again.

Suddenly, the train conductor's voice rang down the corridor, "Attention all passengers, we have reached the final stop in New York City. Please gather your belongings and exit the train in an orderly fashion."

Gordon and Chase looked at each other with relief and disbelief. They had made it to their destination, but they couldn't shake the feeling that they were still in danger. They slowly made their way out of the train car and into the dimly lit station, scanning their surroundings for any sign of the man sent by McGill.

The train station was bustling with people, each one rushing to their next destination. Gordon and Chase tried to blend in with the crowd, but they knew that they were still at risk of being caught. They kept their eyes peeled for any suspicious activity, ready to bolt at the first sign of trouble.

However, even with damning danger lurking behind them, it was impossible not to stare at the beauty of the Grand Central Terminal, which was located at 42nd Street and Park Avenue in Midtown Manhattan.

The Grand Central Terminal was a massive, Beaux-Arts-style building, which featured a monumental limestone, façade with a central clock tower flanked by two large wings.

Inside, the station was even more impressive. The main concourse was a vast, cathedral-like space, with a vaulted ceiling that soared 125 feet above the floor. The ceiling was painted a deep blue color and adorned with constellations of stars, giving the impression that passengers were standing under a starry sky.

The walls of the concourse were covered in white marble, and the floor was made of Tennessee pink marble. The space was flooded with natural light from the massive windows that lined the walls, and the air was filled with the sounds of train whistles and the bustle of passengers.

"You there!" a voice rang out into the crowd.

Gordon and Chase spun around to see the cowboy weaving his way through mounds of people towards them with one goal in mind.

Both men panicked, their eyes darting frantically as they scanned the busy concourse.

Gordon and Chase frantically pushed their way through the crowded train station, trying to lose the cowboy hot on their heels. The sound of his boots pounding against the marble floors echoed through the bustling terminal, drawing curious looks from the other passengers.

As they weaved their way through the throngs of people, Gordon and Chase couldn't help but bump into a few of them, earning them scowls and harsh words from the irritated commuters. They had to navigate around countless obstacles, from overstuffed luggage to groups of tourists snapping selfies in the middle of the walkway.

Despite the chaos around them, they never let up their pace. They dodged through the crowds, turning corners and darting down alleys, always keeping an eye on their pursuer. He was closing in on them, and they could hear his breaths getting louder and more ragged with each passing moment.

The cowboy was ruthless in his pursuit, shoving aside anyone who got in his way. His eyes were locked on Gordon and Chase, his gun at the ready. The two men could feel the weight of his gaze bearing down on them, as if he was daring them to try and get away.

Bursting into the crowded streets of New York, with the cowboy still in pursuit, Gordon and Chase felt despair take over. The noise and chaos of the city made it difficult to hear anything over the din of carriages and shouting vendors, but they could hear the clacking of the cowboy's boots echoing behind them.

People turned to stare as they ran by, but Gordon and Chase paid them no mind. They were focused on finding a place to hide, somewhere that the cowboy wouldn't be able to find them. They weaved through the throngs of people, dodging carts and carriages as they went.

Suddenly, Chase skidded to a stop. "This way!" he shouted, pointing down a narrow alley between two tall buildings. Gordon followed without hesitation, and they both raced into the shadows.

The alley was dimly lit, and the smell of garbage and urine filled the air. But it was a welcome respite from the noise and crowds of the city. Gordon and Chase pressed themselves against the wall, panting for breath as they listened for the sound of the cowboy's footsteps.

But all they could hear was their own heavy breathing. They knew they couldn't stay in the alley forever. They needed to find a way to lose the cowboy for good. Without another word, they pushed off the wall and headed deeper into the alley, looking for a way out.

To Be Continued

Made in the USA
Monee, IL
08 November 2023

45989168R00046